Street Rat

StreetRat

by
Macklin Finley

Greenroom Press
in association with the University of Detroit Mercy

Library of Congress Card Catalog Number: 97-94737
ISBN 0-9661463-1-X
Manufactured in the United States of America

Cover photograph by Anna Culik
Back cover photograph by Chris McCann

StreetRat is dedicated to Greg, Susie, and Maddie, my biggest supporters, and also to my friend, Chris McCann.

"Fugue of the Street Rat" is dedicated to the memory of Tigger, a wise traveller.

Table of Contents

Gutter Punks: A Foreword by John Sinclair 9

The Poetry of Critique: An Introduction 11

Part One

In Gray Eyes 15

Water and Light: a Reflection 17

A Cloud Over Thirteenth 19

Cory 20

After Parting 24

Ending Lies 26

Doc Holliday 30

To Those Who Contemplate Jazz Lyricism 35

Momentary Redemption: A Prayer 40

Smoke in the Garden: A Prayer 41

The Skylight: A Prayer 42

Glad 44

Club-Footed Romeo 46

Shy 53

Part Two

Fugue of the Street Rat 61

I first met Mack Finley at the Clover Grill in New Orleans. The Clover, conveniently situated at 900 Bourbon Street, corner of Dumaine, just three blocks toward the Mississippi River from the former J&M recording studio on Rampart & Dumaine where Dave Bartholomew and Cosimo Matassa made some of the greatest recordings of the 20th century, is what you might call a classic American diner with a twist: it's owned and operated by some of the most flamboyant characters in North America, who cook up and serve the most satisfying plates of eggs with hash browns or grits to be found anywhere, and big juicy hamburgers grilled to perfection under the protective cover of automobile hubcaps.

Sort of a Crescent City/Motown junction in that regard (and several others), the Clover is managed by our mutual friend and poetic colleague, Brad Sumrall, who introduced me to Mack Finley as a fellow expatriate from the Motor City. One night Brad took Mack and me to his hometown, Hattiesburg, Mississippi, where we performed an evening of music and verse in the decrepit, broken down lobby of a former downtown hotel, now taken over as living and working space by artists and weirdoes of every description. We were backed up by a motley collection of skilled and amateur musicians playing everything from tenor saxophone to the guts of an old piano propped up vertically against the wall where it could be pounded upon by an exuberant, would-be player.

During his brief sojourn in the Crescent City, during which he was gainfully employed as an interviewer of "gutter punks" for some sort of post-modern demographic study, Mack also appeared as the ultimate French Quarter street rat who read his poetry for tourists and passersby on Bourbon Street. One year, during the Mardi Gras festivities, Mack performed his works on the street for three days straight, stopping only to puff a quick joint, have a drink and a bite, or relieve himself in the colorful commode at the Clover, and netted from his artistic labors the unbelievable sum of $7,500—every penny of which was quickly confiscated by government authorities seeking satisfaction of a long-ignored tax debt.

I really enjoy Mack Finley's poetry, both on the page and delivered on stage in his distinctive performance style. He casts the experiences and materials of life into verse, quite graceful verse, and he *finds out things* while he's composing, which is a little-heralded but most happy by-product of the writing process. "You wave the first word," as the great Charles

Olson put it, "and the whole thing follows." I started out to write a poem one night about how much I missed my former companion because she'd been "gone so long," in the words of the Professor Longhair song, and by the time I was in the middle of the verse I was asking her to marry me! I had no idea! And the great thing is, we've been happily married ever since. Or, as Mack says:

Declaration of self is the foundation of personal free.
Declaration of self realizes self in all.
Self in all, demands all in self.

It is simple.
The thought of it is no more harrowing than a smile.

That's right: "It is simple." Mack's work will bring a smile to your face, a flash of perception to your brain, and maybe put a little lilt in your step. It might even make you want to dance. Go ahead, it's all right—and can't nobody stop you.

John Sinclair
New Orleans
January 21, 2000

The poetry of the postwar — and "the war" is still the Euro-Asian-American war of the 1940s —inhabits the rubble of cherished beliefs. In the war's aftermath lie the dead, the memory of dying, and the burnt facades of what had been imagined as the eternal city. Gone is certainty and transcendence, and in their place lie probability and immanence. We meet few people as we scramble through the ruins and count corpses, but our deepest suspicions are reserved for the notion of authenticity. Authenticity marked the absolute faith and commitment of the fascists, the Stalinists, the Blueshirts, Brownshirts, and the Father Coughlins. Authenticity imparted a spiritual aura to their sadism, and gave them the confidence to do evil. Infected with what William Burroughs termed "the right virus" they fed our need for certainty until a gangrenous nostalgia erupted. Our unease with such certainty serves as a sort of vaccine against one kind of sin, but it opens us to paralysis, silence, and solipsism. Between these two threats walk poets like Macklin Finley.

In the Beats, this unease with authenticity opened poetry to Buddhism, to taboo sexualities, and to a politics that recognized that the great wheel of Time-Fortune-Life had acquired a copyright and a board of directors. Poetry's inward eye turned itself toward essential identities; its outer eye passed moral judgment on the thousand dead cityscapes that surround us. It has been a complex counterpointing of deep cultural skepticism against the individual integrity that drives the poet to assert poems. In short, the massive dangers of authenticity offer themselves as an argument for silence, for the empty page, for emptying out the garret where the poet is supposed to write.

Between the dangers of fascistic control and autistic solipsism, the poet's task becomes increasingly more complex. Macklin Finley's poetry bespeaks this quandary, and it does so as the poetry of critique, a poetry that — to borrow religious words — is "in" but not "of" the world. Finley's book begins with poems written out of individual, idiosyncratic experience, the experiences of love, of loss, of anxiety. But these poems are built of imagery that reemerges in the later poems. The images reemerge to create the cityscapes, the adolescent streetrats, the preying police and the predatory patriarchs cruising for a boy to cap off their night. These images dispossess us of certainty, of transcendence, and of the absolute moral judgment that can grow and fester and mutate into an as yet

11

unimagined fascism. Finley never flinches from his own carefully situated emotion, nor does he deny us the camaraderie of dispossession in all its forms. But just as fiercely, he contains his vision *as* the vision of a single poet, albeit one with all the social and moral sensibilities of his Beat predecessors.

So why is Macklin Finley worth reading? My answer is simple: he insists that we see the world of the streetrat, of the dispossessed child, the dispossessed lover, and even of the poets who have been dispossessed of faith and certainty but who have made a newer and more complex poetry out of our condition. They — and especially Macklin Finley — are the poets of critique.

Josef Kurtz
Detroit
March 5, 2000

PART ONE

A starboard
tie frost.

A kettle in west
blowing storm.

Spreading paper
blowing
endless gray.

No constellation prizes:
one comes late,
a structure falls.

The glass rattling
the wind;
shhh...
shhh...

June-fabulous misconceptions,
a hot blue with
wayward walks.

All in dust, waiting,
registering complaints of neglect,

The moon reflects
the lake.

Green   going
Gray   coming.

Unseasonable.

By West Nine, rolling.
Through the temple, rolling.

Until unrolled;
    a red carpet spreads
    blood feast for
    bent beggars.

The woods no more,
      pagan feast in
      park 'n' go diners.
The coffee girl, slim of hip
      fleet of thought
      still smiling.
Holding the recognition of
      all of this
      at bay.

Starboard tie frost
      waiting.
      All of this,
nothing more.
The storm waits,
the children teach
the old not to
care.

Water and Light: a Reflection

A boy sits
alone on
the bank
of the
Huron.

He has
retreated
out of
youth's
physicality
into
a truer self
that he will
always
un-know.

Light
refracts
reflects
on the
water.

The water
reflects the
light and
passes
unchanged.

The boy
stands
and walks.

Youth resumes
at the
park gate.

Un-know
becomes
a void
he does not
carry with him.

Paralytic confusion settles
over a small room.
>Welcome to my life,
>says a lesser poet
>with his head unhinged.
>A pyre of capital in his veins.
>>A man with no
>>discernible chin
>>smugly reads Rimbaud
>>in the comer,
>>>oblivious.
The ambivalent bystanders pace quietly away.
The professor alights
the chair, with sudden
anger,
Screaming.
>His tirade is delivered in Latin,
>and, without footnotes,
>the room only registers more noise.
>>The lesser poet,
>>still so affected,
>>adjusts his head
>>and leaves the
>>room.
>>>Classics, he thinks,
>>>are another escape
>>>from death.
>>>The people,
>>>shows the poet to himself
>>>never outlive their words.

Three pennies
fall like
rain in
the thunderous
silence after.

Remorse is
a court word
holding no
tender in the
lives of
men.

As one
more chokes
into the
nameless
void and
one more
skirts
St. Claude
outside the
street
light.

Eyes not
guilty,
but
free will
be blessed
with the
splendor
of another
southern
dawn.

We stand
on the
corner
amidst
the buzz
the flow
their cash
inextractable.

The flow
on which
we prey
which
invariably
covers us in
a film
of spilled
broken
bottles.

The heat
has descended.
Surely another
night will
follow, long,
sleepless,
dusty.

How many
have been
lost?
How many
mothers'
sons
choke
gasp
and
die

as
three pennies
fall like
rain in
the thunderous
silence
after?

The conversational
undulations
of the
literate class
reverberate
off three a.m.
floorboards—
Determining
ideology
idiotically—
A quarter
mile away
the bookless,
stoic,
brave,
die—
without
words
to calm
         them.

A quarter mile
away
choice
is a
distant
dream,
a vague recollection—
somethin'
t'get

to.

We walk
a fine
line
down
Rampart's median,
unwanted
on either
side.

Nothing can
be done
as
three pennies
fall like
rain in
the thunderous
silence
after.

1.

Can only learn through pain.
Living by painting extravagant shadows to hide in.

A pretty girl sits on a brick wall.
Smiles hello. Offers company. Possibly more.
Old wounds run deep. I can not speak.

A tree grows in my soul. It turns to ash
in the wind.

I would strike my tongue for spite but can
not find it.

Dog flowers in tin cans: I have no plans.

2.

The sky rolls, forward.
Surprises itself
from behind.

Shrieks, spits, flashes.

Shy and mighty.
Unending to begin again.
Ending to begin being.

3.

"Find yourself a dive bar,"
The prophets say
through rotten teeth
as they sip sugar water
from shot glasses.

They tip out and the band
strikes up their ancient

march.

Dionysius tends bar. Sober county;
he serves sugar water and gasoline.

"Too many prophets," he says, "standing room only."

5.

I would be gray but bend to red.
I would be red but am sustained in blue.
I would be gray.

Who is the voice through night panic?
No one. There is no one there at all.
Who holds the warmth?
No one. There is no one there at all.

6.

Old wounds run deep. I can not speak.

A statue in memoriam has built
itself in my throat.

Have lost the ability to feel pain.
Can only learn through pain.

Dog flowers in tin cans: I have no plans.

7.

It does not matter. Coffee pots shatter.
A sickly yellow floor.

An orange couch. A lie we told.

You will be broken by those sticks you carry.
When you draw up a dark burgundy swirl
you will disappear into it and snap to be
heard.

1.
This history is meaningless.
All of the finer points have been
stamped out in
full parade marching drills.

They govern us in
weather patterns.
But a citizen does not
fall from perfect
infantile innocence,
through
ferocious childhood
and sinister adolescence,
to adulthood,
to sitting in a chair
waiting to die,
without
becoming a person
along the way.

The plasticine
        aristocratic social devils
have won.
They fill the shelves
with so many books
about
who we should be,
who they are,
and what it means to be,
that most of us
decide not to see.

They tie us off.
Separate solitary Timon,
to our solitary woodlands

to suffer under a sky
rent with storms of
hollow epiphany.

The great clouds
of society.

Most of us decide
not to decide.

They made flags,
so they could tell us
what it means.
But, by the time
they finished teaching
us all the lyrics
to all the
Torahs
and
Korans
and
bibbles
and
baublesome
little rhetoric
about black cats,
pennysides, and
fiddlers dancing on graves,
we couldn't possibly have
cared.

So we don't.

We stare in gape-mouthed
reverie, as they move in,
chain us down, and
give us mortgage
applications and welfare

referendums and
movie screens.
We stand here waiting.
Slack mouthed starving
eunuchs, woefully
destroying whatever
trinkets we can lay
hand to as
an expression of
sullen revenge
and hopeless
acquiescence.

2.

    Above it all,
        there's this
    beautiful sky.

    I pray you listen,
    as I call:

                I'm caught,
                brother,
                I'm hung down.
                Chained. Owned.
                My voice doesn't
                reach far,
                and I can't speak
                too long.
                But our four
                hands together
                could break two
                chains this strong.
                No generals are
                needed to strike up
                a march.
                Just us,
                just us, going the same

way.
Let's just move with
a wink, and a nod.
Let's see who winds
up on top, when we
pull the top down.

3.
That, that is, lies within.

Declaration of self is the foundation of personal free.
Declaration of self realizes self in all.
Self in all, demands all in self.

It is simple.
The thought of it is no more harrowing than a smile.

1.

Doc Holliday
spat a little
shriveled lung in
his kerchief,
straightened
his hat—
found the next
whiskey—
savored the
irony.

His boots
were always
shined to
a bright
black glow—
matching
his eyes.

He was a
wizard
of a kind.
He was a
wizard
way ahead
of his time.
Doc Holliday
was wise
to the
plans of
the other man—
Doc Holliday
was wise
to the
deck in

hand—
Doc Holliday
was wise
to the
street
before there
was a
street to
be wise
    to.

2.

Doc Holliday
stood—thin—
shakin' in the
too hot sun—
He was dying
and he knew
it didn't
matter—
the country was
growing—
modernizing.
He would be
an anecdote—
    if he made
    it that
    far—
The sun
formed
slow
bubbles in
his eyes.
A fifteen year old
kid stood a
hundred paces downwind—
A drunken bet
was the cause.

Draw Squeeze—
One shot
a body falls—
A boy died
in the street.
It did not
matter.
Doc Holliday's
next drink's
free—the fever
worse—he sweats
through his sportcoat—
Saw white horses
ridin' high in
strange black
streets—eerie humming
glowing signs
in impossible
windows.
Children squatting
on stone walks
near the black
patch—their
hands out,
their eyes
dead—odd
bruises, scabs
tracing their
veins thumping
in unison—
Cough shakes
him to—

Praised be the
vision of our murderous
father, Doc Holliday.

3.

There's a
kid down the
way
with a finger
in every pie—
He's got
old style
hustle
with his
hat on.
Majesty
is nothin' but
practice for
comfort;
the boy's
a king of
unthinkable
consequence
makin' it
work—
Night to
night, day
to day.
He's gotta
take care of
the shit
that gotta
be taken
care of—
So when
a boy dies
on the
paved streets
of modern day
America—
Everyone knows
it does not

matter.
Boy/king
'round the
corner
lights a
candle
on the
altar for
every soul
he brings down
in grim street
light.

Tripping
    falling
        constantly
            stalling.

Waiting
    for a voice
    to shine
    through the
    night.

The voice never
    calls,
'cept in a
voice we don't
    hear,
    to a name
we don't
    recognize.

I'm kinda
    blue,
    and,
Miles will
    blow,
but it never
takes me home.

Bmt-dn-ndna,
        so what?

So who was Miles,
    and what issue
    gets offed in
    his pursuit?

He just played
     to get played,
         right?

Bmt-dn-ndna,
         so what?

So that's why
     it was fine
     for him
     to stumble in
     wearing a
     heroin negligee
     while Eldridge Cleaver
     got thrown in a
     cage for a bag
     of pot.

Is that right?

Eldridge never
     played
     for anyone;
he never got
played on
nor played out.

The people waiting
     to be played for,
just wouldn't have that.

The Jazzy mad
     publishing gurus
     saw ways through
     integral voice,
         in loophole formations.
Stumbled through the door,
     right after death.

Screaming,
    "Dig it, wow."
Screaming
    mad rhetoric
    and jazz climaxes.

Then they left.
    Laughing all
    the way
    to the bank.

Cashing in the
    radical readers' loftier
    intentions.

In the hip
    bank for new
    'with-it' money
    the speakers
    were blaring,
    BLARING Miles.

Bmt-dn-ndna,
    so what?

So jazz happened
and was had.
The beat played
on
    and nothing
    was allowed
    to happen
    again.

Undercurrent
jazz leaders, now
where did they
go?

                    Just down the
                    street,
                    to the studio.

So what,
        so who plays
        what for whom,
        and what does
        it mean to them
        when they,
                do it?
Money?
        Power?
                Fame?
                        Delusion,
Sun Ra Alabama
alien uprising.
        Claiming Miles his idol,
        even from way back on Mars.

Suburban Acid kids
everywhere, dying to get
on the scene.
Twitching at the
ticket counter with
a pocket full of
daddy's money
and a gallon of
orange juice.
        "Space is the
                place,
                man."

Sun Ra should've
listened to
Gil-Scot Heron.
on space,

"A rat done bit
my sista Nell,
and whitey's
on the moon."

Sun Ra very
        safe,
there in
        space,
never meaning
anything.

Momentary Redemption: A Prayer

A tool maker
sees stars shine.

A glass ceiling
falling between
himself and the sky,
the sky
rife with so
many jewels.

Cursing all the luck,
until ginful
and wonder-eyed,
the clouds roll
back.

Lips numb with prayer
and laced with blasphemy,
trace the arch.

It's all been wind-shine
beneath a thought shackle.

A tree in the backyard.
Now the old men
standing in brick circles
tell us,
"Imagine it suffering."

Who can?
No one,
so it's bar-b-que
talk.
Something to say
on someone
else's patio.

These things
become tools.
The words
Fly out in daily
speech forming
what can be
described
as a man
as a woman.

The Skylight: A Prayer

Stars shine
bright
but half
the
night.
The other
half blinking.

They carry
cross the
spatial tide.

The ability
to look out
and see them
is not a
survival
technique.
It is an
aesthetic
sense.

What a thought
was had.

Hidden like
a pearl in
the silent
face of
infinity.

That was had
and had itself,
then subdivided
and was had
only to have

again.

How I love
to live to
be its tool,
for it is all
a gear.
That turns
and winds up

in patio sunshine
speech.
Or is found
on the walks
taken aimlessly
to nowhere.

Glad

Does my name
sound different
on your lips
now that I'm
not with you?

Does the water
miss the sun
it has reflected
when it passes
underground?

Do the voices
of happy people
fill you with
shame for all
the time we
wasted pretending
to be like
them?

I've never loved,
only feared loneliness.

I sit in crowded places
alone
until they empty
and I must
accept the
solitary state.

I don't mind it
as much,
now that I
have the
comparison

of your
company.

The lessons of
silence are
now open
to me.

Spent morning wrapped
in others' vacuous
conversation, like
dead fish stained in
ink of yesterday's
'why bother' headlines—
One bearded sausage link
in ill-fitting, double breasted,
navy discomfort, spoke
of the foreignization
of the professoriate.
And, had he dropped
the fifty cent lingo
du jour, his long-nosed,
parrot-faced
wife may have
realized she'd
been sleeping with
a bigot. Though,
she probably
wouldn't have
cared—

And this Roseanne
look-a-like drag
queen who'd been
buying me coffee
for five hours,
started wind-bagging
about connections
of this kind and that—
Ever seen a neutered
poodle hump a
potted plant?
That was absolutely
the look—

Parrot woman
digs her Pinkie Lee
Press-On nail into
her left nostril; she's
praying nobody'll
notice, and I'm
praying that the
hot pink plastic
will come unglued
so deeply imbedded
that the bearded walrus,
whose collar stays
must be digging
cute little holes
in his breast
plate, will have
to dislodge it
with his butter knife—

So the cafe fades
like first-act trappings.
I'm moving through the
caramel-scented street,
a club-footed Romeo
selecting engagements
with rings unfit for
fingers. And Juliet
seems so far out
of time in the
disaster-ridden
street light—
More like Ophelia
bathing in dim glow
than a tall woman
jaywalking just a
block from home.
        Home,

Which is mutual
in its ill-fated
clean-up attempts.
In all my
bitter vagary,
I give her a
puerile impression
and, on suited
knee, present a
silver band
which squats
narrowly on her
thumb.

I meet her
drinking coffee
on her day's
wage, in a
diner more
home than
stained bed sheets.
While the handsome
cook whispers
in my right
ear of herbal
essence, she
counts chicken
feet tips into
my left hand.

Just a club-footed
Romeo
everywhere I
go, tripping
over sidewalk
cracks, spilling
my brains like
Scrabble cubes

on the pavement
where they tell
the pretty little
story of timid
eye contact
and injurious
miscommunication.

In his room,
thick with
smoke, he
pronounces breathless
verses saying,
"But for
this I would sing in
praise of gentle curving
smiles."

Wondering if only
my mind carries
a brooding seductive
nature. My promise
already lies like
undyed linen in
an unmade bed.
The tint of
gold in otherwise
oaken linings.

I flood
home with
gutter feelings
in a muddy olive
suit, completing
conversations of
bystanders,
judging rhythm
of heels

clicking in
echoes of
"this bar was
built by
so-and-so."
Transforming
minimum-wage
beer and wet
rag day shifts
into idyllic
tourist "look
how they
live" imagery.
And my stomach's
    gurgling last
night's indiscretion,
hoping tonight's
temptation falls
onto lily petal
ears as lightly,
and in learned
maternal preparatory
instinct and
Freudian slipology,
teeth and
gums to minty
deception, wondering
what odor
needs covering:
Billiards or
unrequited longing—

I am solemn
in quest for
warmth of her
limbs and tongue
rapture devoiding
doubting nature

of shiny shoes
in soft rainfall
of deserted streets
and half-shell
fed mustaches
in full swagger
treading stones
in my wake,
wantful pursuit,
maybe?

The rue is
all sharks, and
the young, sliding,
sidewinder pedestrians
are plump surf-
board swimmers
in disquieted
repose.

Dumaine smells
of home,
but I dig gentleman's
pocket for
onion change
and witness
the diner's
shift switch
and, in steam,
see maudlin
masks of
theater frown
and smile in
dusk left and
right dichotomy,
and the Act One
dialogue
splays doggedly

in younger tones,
talking unanimity
at brush strokes
of toast-butter.

shy

Woke up
in catastrophe
apartment, unaware
of night activities.
Took a last
stab at Bourbon St.,
faced all her consequences;
the whole city's
hungover,
    dying—
The gutter's
full of liquor
and ten thousand
tourists'
paper
cup dreams.
By the
dawn's early
light, I am
fading into
the sidewalk
like yesterday's
chalk of some
vandal's runaway
dream.
I am haunted
by the voice
of love's last
night confession,
how she bent
to tempting
sympathy
because she
was so
long ago
"just too shy."

I hide behind
tough twitches,
sunglasses,
and an
unfiltered
voice.
I will
always carry
echoing, feminine
voices.
Something
about this shattering,
dawn walk
leads me
to believe
the sun on
the dead
buildings
will reignite
long dead
hope.
Sudden turning
to the river
I wish I
was strong
enough to
drown in—
But better
pens have
painted
its brown
madness
pretty—
They killed
the Mississippi
and stomped
all over its
smooth drawl—

The more
I know
the South,
the more
I ache
for home.

I was just
too shy
to ever
do or
say the
right thing.
So a timid
virgin went
down in flames
while being
chased by
a deep brown,
Mexican
horse—
She didn't
scream or
fight, and
ten stories
were more
than plenty
to render
her limp and
lifeless.

Timid, little,
tough girl
struggles
for the
love of
a barred-in
street king,

and I guide
her to the
bottle-gets-
y'to-the-
backroom
bars—
Talking
of bail,
she goes
down on
Hope,
and I am just
too shy
to tell
her that
Hope is
for Hollywood.

The only
one that
ever
mattered
waits,
protruding;
a baby
breathes
between
her belly
and her lap—
And I
tell her
we can
do it,
together,
but every
face informed
shakes—
And I am

not a
father
figure—
How well
we know
the words,
but settling
into a
room rendered
gray and
smoky
by too
many
hangers-on,
I am just
too shy.

PART TWO

Movement 1.

Some try to sleep it off
in the late-night
holding cells,
norelativestocall,
no bail to be posted.
Some stand and pace,
bitter stomachs
and torn minds
toiling against broken
stamina.
What next? What next?
Bullshit tournaments in
the corner—
Who's the baddest?
In this last-stop
dead-end cell he
with loudest voice
is booming his
notorious command—
"You be my bitch in the house."
And it's misplaced anger
for that last five minutes
of out time
that went so
wrong.
There will be a change.

Movement 2.

I've spent six years
pouring sand
into a coffee cup,
watching it overflow
and add character
to otherwise sterile
free verse.

In an induced dream
I was kept at the
bottom of a well
that filled in
icy purity around
me—and all the
while, mice died
in the bare lightbulbs
miles overhead.

Another head splits
under the thrust
of a billy club,
another wrong-looker
goes down for this or
that—and a right-looking
wrongdoer violates
the trusting nature
of a street rat,
'round the comer,
knowin' he doesn't
have a thing to
fear.

Movement 3.
Nights that plague
reality, poking holes
in it, setting it
to purple flames
of delusion—
Mystified, pinned
on walls in pale
street lights—
passing smiles in
choking voiceless
rooms and unconscious
connections

forming lines
at money burners
Begging for a little
escape
(fast set down
fast money
for fast connections).
Itching at the corners:
Escape! Escape!
Making kissing noises
at the passing faces—
Gotta pay somehow—
need a ride—
need a bed—
need a hot, hairy, middle-aged
hand on your thigh—
"Cause you look a little
cold, and I could use a
little company."
That little wedding ring
don't mean a damn thing 'cause
I can buy out the sentiment
behind it.
Besides, if it's not you it's
some other beer-starved
mouth.
You need the fix,
po' white trash, nigga,
spic, queer, li'l boy with
no one to talk with, and
no bed to sleep in, never
mind your confused sexuality—
I gotta big green paper
dick for you to suck on—
and once you have, you can
get high.
Won't that be nice?
Wake up, middle-aged

whore monger,
there will be a great day
of reckoning.

Movement 2, part 2.
She tells me the
whole
oddly familiar story,
of awkward/hostile
advances and the
smell of money.
She wanted to
strike a blow,
but deep inside
she has the
wisdom of peace.
Says she has
respect for her elders;
she pours narrative
onto my plate,
where it forms a bitter
stew.
The cook's peering
at us from the corner
of his eye like
every rebel in every
rebel movie—
And two cash-soaked
businessmen point
at us saying
"Derelicts."
I've spent six
years trying to
be something more,
and there will be
a change.

Movement 3, part 2.

Young and poor—
No god to pray to—
No luck to pray for—
Nothin' but life chokin'
on life.
So, whatcha in for?
Calls it "Public drunk," not
doin' a damn thing. Jus'
walkin', but the th' cop go's
me figured on a diff'rent
score—
Who ain't in the central
for jus' bein' bo'n?
Who ain't?

Around the little yellow
brick room with varying
shades of criminal elementation
DUIs—WIFE BEATERS—KICK
BACKSTOOPDRUNKS—DRAGON
CHASERS—SLICKED BACK
SILK SHIRT SLY TALKERS—
Guilty men—Innocent men—
Men betrayed by a system
that told them they were free.

Young and poor
No god to pray to—
No luck to pray for—
Nothin' but life chokin'
on life.
So, whatcha in for?

Movement 4.

So, who am I?
is there an "I" that stands
out as more than a cog

in this rusty old machine?
Who Am I—
Who Am I—
Who Am I?
Am I the junk in veins—
The wine in skin—
An inebriate forming
consciousness cocktails—
scotch and soda handcuffs?
Happy Hour
Happy Hour—
3 for 1 Happy Hour—
Who wants sanity—
Who wants sobriety?

Neon-rendered
Uncle Sam points
fingers at fine
foreign slaughters
and I know—
I know who
doesn't.
Corporation
America with its
indirect democracy
has bred a
quarter generation
of dead-end
addicts;
the children beg
your spare
change for
alcohol—spare
change for
alcohol.

Give this generation
an uncoated tongue.

We will do what the
hippies sold out on.
Give this generation
one night, one night
to come up sober,
and we will change
these things that
have been done.

Chorus 1
I find my definition
in storm patterns—
A change of energy.
I can feel it underfoot—
the sky is flecked
light with grey.
I think I may
feel partly
cloudy.
Like a thunderclap
I am deafening in
fierce self-proclamations.
Like the sky I am poisoned
by industry; the city's smokestacks
choke me, and the five o'clock
traffic jam is burning
holes in me with its
bitter exhaust.

I think I may—
I think I may—
feel partly cloudy.

And I don't want to
be a rain of history
on your day-in-the-park parade—
but I'm vaporous, controlled by
the elements raining

heard words on deaf
ears—you're walking
down a street of gutter
punks, starving,
wise children,
coast to coast wanderers—
and all this pretty extravagance
has been hung on poles of
degradation: for your benefit.
Somebody tell the children
with their fiddle stories
and longtime bad habits,
that these neon beer
gardens are cesspools
of wasted minds
and lives of no
reward.

I think I may—
I think I may—
feel partly cloudy.

Movement 5.
Hey, mid-line easy
solution conservatives,
it's time to
light another flare
of audacious contempt,
honesty is for those
too weak to invent
a history of
victory:

Fall into goose-step
formation
Horatio Alger.
These porch-step
children

starve for your
legacy,
and those in
steadfastly
full states and
sensible
shoes bypass with
biting
remarks.

Emotion is for the gays,
the artists, and other
enemies of the state.
Callous is the
call to arms for anybody
with anything to
speak of.
And poverty?
"Poverty
is a rising tide of laziness."

So rise to the
occasion
heads of state,
there's a new
generation
to screw over,
and they're too
atrophied to resist.
All it should take
is the offer of
a Big Mac to pull
them into line.
Or a simple co-optation
of their heroes,
maybe.
Bend this generation
and

pump them
hard with their MTV
reality.
There is no
movement,
and just look how
hard
you banged the baby
boomers
with theirs.

Welcome to zero
tolerance
G money. There are
greater
punishments than
death
for pride in the
New World Order.
Our march will
overtake
you and all these
malcontents who
would
dare difference.

Fall into goose step
formation, Horatio
Alger;
the New World Order
needs you.

Movement 1, part 2.
Inside Inside Inside
The horror stories get
laid on thick.
Fourteen year old kid in
under two different

70

adult names for
two different crimes
he didn't commit.
They wonder where the hopelessness comes in at
the universities—
Inside Inside Inside
They move this fourteen-year-
old kid from
cell to cell wrapped in chains
once a week—
Two crimes
    Two adult names,
Robert Jameson Jr.
please hear me:
They've got a chain
for your ankles,
They've got a chain
for your wrists.
Nobody, nobody
has a chain for your mind.
Talks to me on the
lock down bench,
heard my bail'd come up.
Story alien
to my way of life—
walkin' home from school
stopped for a bag
search. Seems
a near daily affair,
walkin' home from
school, gettin' searched,
smart-ass
remark—
arrested him on the
spot
for two crimes
they knew he didn't
commit, two adult

names they knew
weren't his,
an intentional wrench
in a rusty machine.
This is zero tolerance.
He tells me his family
will be waiting outside.
They are. I tell them—
He's okay. No one's pickin' on
him—
I don't tell them, he's
questioning why he was a
good student, why he
went to church;
I don't tell them
that turned loose,
he may be a real criminal—
But then—
from their eyes,
they already know.

Movement 3, part 3.
Lobotomizing without tools,
tubes in noses,
paper on tongues—
Constant escape,
circular streets
around and down,
scraping gutters,
sleeping in abandoned homes
watchful of peripheral motion—
Always taking chances
with motions like
a train.
Needles in veins
Needles in veins
Needles in veins.
Pink blood, diluted

blood, blocking the
works blood, cramming the
artery blood. Metallic tastes
numb tongues, prickly eyes
watery walls—
unaware a thousand
tomorrows rusty machines
around like turnstile justice.
Like a train rhythm—money
burning—like a train rhythm—
bondsmen and pushers
bondsmen and pushers
bondsmen and pushers—

Insane on floors—
Spinning—Hot Hairy Middle-
Aged hands—Gotta pay somehow—
like a train rhythm:
Shaking at dawn
for another,
another,
another.

Movement 6.

Living on broken bread-crust
promises—
Telling her I'll be
fine.
Struggling to get a
foothold outta bed—
Bleak—slow—blurry—
No comfort—itching
at the comers—
Struggling for control
of the headboard—
You can't have it
'till you cut me—
Red/brown bed sheets,

grinding—in/out
sweating/reeling/
needing/releasing
gentle song
neighbors complaining
springs—
Needing—itching at
the corners—confusing
desires—wanting—metallic
tastes.
Needing
Needing
Needing
Hot Hairy Middle-Aged
Hands
Gotta pay—
Gotta pay somehow—
Is there an "I"—
Am I all that I am?
I want to keep the promises,
but, y'see there's this
train rhythm.

Chorus 2.

There will be a change—
It'll take time—
It took 220 years
for one nation to
fall this far.
There will be a
great day of reckoning.
It won't be biblical in nature.
It will be fueled
on street rat blood.
We will roll down
the gutters and
paint your uptown
condos red.

There will be
as little mercy
as possible.
Your Romanesque
capitols and monuments
will fall about
your presidential
myths
like the levied
pound of flesh.
There will be
a great day of
reckoning.
Caste-system
education
will burn
and tumble
on pretty
blonde pep rallies—
dunce cap
wrong trackside
bag search children
will wipe
their names
from the board—
education—humiliation
forced into drop-
out situation—
Teacher, teacher,
get ready for graduation.

Movement 2, part 3.

Phone call to
Chairman Mao—
cultural clean-up committee.
Street sweep silk swine,
ROTC—make matters matter
enlist socialist.

ROTC—make matters matter
kill the corporal.
ROTC—make matters matter;
Who wants sanity—
Who wants sobriety—
Not neon rendered
Uncle Sam—

Phone call to
Abbie Hoffman—
Yippie—bygone
clean-up committee—
tie-dye mini-vans,
pour Monopoly money
on stock scene
desk junky—
runaway cultural
highbrow.
ROTC—make matters matter
enlist anarchist.
ROTC—make matters matter
drop out.
ROTC—make matters matter
Who wants sanity—
Who wants sobriety—
Kill the corporal.

Phone call to Che Guevara,
Don't cry for me,
clean-up committee Trotsky,
Close third-world casinos,
Time-magazine
bankruptcy. Runaway
street-martyr death-scene
doctor motorcycle diary.
ROTC—make matters matter—
head for radio waves.
ROTC—make matters matter

head for mountains.
ROTC—make matters matter
select new corporal.
Sanity sobriety
SHAZAAM!
Brand-new
Uncle SAM!

Chorus 3.

In and out
dusty phone booths
dying young with bad lookin'
yellow, inflated corpses.
Dusty back-alleys
risks like a train rhythm,
needles in veins
needles in veins
needles in veins
blood wash spoon
nicotine
chasers
there will be a change.
Gotta pay—born in debt—hot
hairy—Clorox clean-up
committee—phone call
to Jimi/Janis—shot up—
Put down—hung on last
generation's sellout
ambitions—song of
somebody else—
Phone call to Walt Whitman—
Unlisted—sanity—sobriety—
Change—will there be—
Is there an I—change—
Sanity—train rhythm—
Ran risk stop sign—
Clean-up committee—
Zero tolerance—

Heard words—symphony.
Phone call to William
Shakespeare—heard words—
Othello blackface comedy—
downstairs train rhythm—

It's very drug cultury—
I don't know if I can
hang with all the smoke
up in here.

Finale
ROTC—brand new Uncle
Sam Shazaam—change—
sobriety—sanity—make way
symphony street rat.
Cut cultural form—
Myopic runaway vision—symphony—
Street rat—change
Inside—outside
ROTC—phone call—
Needles in veins—
Train rhythm—
Change—dialect—
Information—
Fast money—
Phone call to Allen
Ginsberg—Howl at penthouse
Wall—Dialect change—symphony—
ROTC—ROTC—kill young—money
blood—zero tolerance—verbs
proverbs—symphony—street at—Punk girls crying—
Boyfriends
in jail—Pushers and bondsmen—
Train rhythm—dunce cap—bag
search—brown shirts—turnstile—
Change—symphony—empathy—
Constant motion—circular

streets—living lies like—politicians—
Symphony—street rats—change—
Inside—Inside—Inside—
    Change.

Macklin Finley's childhood dinners were served beneath three emblematic portraits. The first two (Marx and Stalin) soon became only one, but the portrait of Eliot had no competitor. Subsequently and perhaps consequently, Finley's career has been as a poet, but as a poet who inhabited the world of New Orleans' streetrats, the corridors of Detroit's emptied factories and boarded-up neighborhoods. His jobs have included stints as a luggage salesman, dishwasher, busboy, short-order cook, waiter, ice cream scooper, yogurt scooper, and street poet. While working these jobs, he has done his real work as a poet. Recent publications include the *Saturday Afternoon Journal*.